MW00881254

WOUL[D]
RATHER ?

Ewwww!
VERSION

FOLLOW US AT:

 WWW.FACEBOOK.COM/ WOULDYOURATHERBOOK

 @WOULDYOURATHERBOOK

WWW.WOULDYOURATHERBOOK.COM

COME
JOIN OUR GROUP

GET A BONUS PDF PACKED WITH HILARIOUS JOKES, AND THINGS TO MAKE YOU SMILE!

GO TO:

shorturl.at/cdLRT

■ **Get a Bonus fun PDF** (filled with jokes, and fun would you rather questions)

■ **Get entered into our monthly competition to win a $100 Amazon gift card**

■ **Hear about our up and coming new books**

HOW TO PLAY?

You can play to win or play for fun, the choice is yours!

1. Player 1 asks player 2 to either choose questions **A** or **B**.

2. Then player 1 reads out the chosen questions.

3. Player 2 decides on an answer to their dilemma, and either memorize their answer or notes it down.

4. Player 1 has to guess player 2's answer. If they guess correctly they win a point, if not player 2 wins a point.

5. Take turns asking the questions, **the first to 7 points wins.**

(Note: It can be fun to do funny voices or make silly faces)

REMEMBER
Do **NOT** ATTEMPT TO DO ANY OF THE SCENARIOS IN THIS BOOK, THEY ARE ONLY MEANT FOR FUN!

Ewwww! VERSION

PLAYER 1

(ASK THE OTHER PLAYER(S) TO
CHOOSE QUESTION 1 OR QUESTION 2)

A = WOULD YOU RATHER

EAT THE GREEN BOOGER FROM YOUR BEST FRIEND'S NOSE

 OR

eat a big fat cockroach?

B = WOULD YOU RATHER

let a snake sleep in your bed for the night

 OR

Allow a clown to sleep in your bed for the night?

Ewwww! VERSION

PLAYER 2

(ASK THE OTHER PLAYER(S) TO
CHOOSE QUESTION 1 OR QUESTION 2)

A WOULD YOU RATHER

EAT TWO TINS OF CAT FOOD

EAT SOMETHING FROM YOUR BIN?

B WOULD YOU RATHER

SMELL YOUR SMELLIEST FART FOR TEN MINUTES STRAIGHT

SMELL THE FART OF A FAMOUS PERSON FOR FIVE MINUTES?

Ewwww! VERSION

PLAYER 1

(ASK THE OTHER PLAYER(S) TO
CHOOSE QUESTION 1 OR QUESTION 2)

A WOULD YOU RATHER

KISS A FROG

 OR

KISS SOMEONE THAT HAS NOT HAD A BATH FOR A WEEK?

B WOULD YOU RATHER

HOLD A SNAKE

 OR

THROW UP GREEN SLIME?

Ewwww!
VERSION

PLAYER 2

(ASK THE OTHER PLAYER(S) TO
CHOOSE QUESTION 1 OR QUESTION 2)

A WOULD YOU RATHER

SHOWER IN A PLACE THAT SMELT OF PEE

BATH IN A PLACE THAT SMELLED LIKE RAW MEAT?

B WOULD YOU RATHER

YOUR DAD TURNED IN A GIANT PINK MONSTER

YOUR MOM CHANGED INTO A FIERCE LION?

Ewwww!
VERSION

PLAYER 1

(ASK THE OTHER PLAYER(S) TO
CHOOSE QUESTION 1 OR QUESTION 2)

A — WOULD YOU RATHER

EAT A PIZZA COVERED IN WORMS

 OR

A HAMBURGER WITH GRASSHOPPERS ON?

B — WOULD YOU RATHER

LICK THE FLOOR

 OR

DRESS UP AS A HORSE AND GO AROUND TOWN MAKING HORSE NOISES?

Ewwww! VERSION

PLAYER 2

(ASK THE OTHER PLAYER(S) TO
CHOOSE QUESTION 1 OR QUESTION 2)

A = WOULD YOU RATHER

SMELL YOUR TEACHER'S ARMPIT UP CLOSE

DRINK YOUR OWN PEE?

B = WOULD YOU RATHER

GET VERY SICK AND THROW UP PINK MARSHMALLOWS

BE WELL AND RUN FOR AN ENTIRE DAY WITHOUT STOPPING?

Ewwww! VERSION

PLAYER 1

(ASK THE OTHER PLAYER(S) TO
CHOOSE QUESTION 1 OR QUESTION 2)

A WOULD YOU RATHER

DRINK ROTTEN FISH JUICE

 OR

DRINK FROGS SPAWN ?

B WOULD YOU RATHER

EAT A POO FLAVOURED ICE-CREAM

 OR

EAT CHOCOLATE CAKE WITH SNAIL SLIME INSIDE?

Ewwww! VERSION

PLAYER 2

(ASK THE OTHER PLAYER(S) TO
CHOOSE QUESTION 1 OR QUESTION 2)

A — WOULD YOU RATHER

HAVE A GIANT SPIDER CRAWL ON YOUR BACK WHILE YOU ARE SLEEPING

 OR

HAVE A SNAKE SLITHER INTO YOUR BED WHILE YOU ARE SLEEPING?

B — WOULD YOU RATHER

WATCH SCARY MOVIES ALL NIGHT

 OR

WATCH SOPPY LOVE STORIES ALL NIGHT?

Ewwww! VERSION

PLAYER 1

(ASK THE OTHER PLAYER(S) TO
CHOOSE QUESTION 1 OR QUESTION 2)

A — WOULD YOU RATHER

ROLL AROUND IN HORSE POO

 OR

ROLL AROUND IN RABBIT WEE?

B — WOULD YOU RATHER

BE BITTEN BY A ZOMBIE

 OR

BE BITTEN BY A VAMPIRE?

Ewwww! VERSION

PLAYER 2

(ASK THE OTHER PLAYER(S) TO
CHOOSE QUESTION 1 OR QUESTION 2)

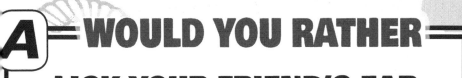

WOULD YOU RATHER

A

LICK YOUR FRIEND'S EAR WAX

OR

LICK YOUR GRANDMOTHER'S FOOT?

WOULD YOU RATHER

B

TURN INTO A FROG FOR THE REST OF YOUR LIFE

OR

LIFE AS A BIRD FOR THE REST OF YOUR LIFE?

Ewwww! VERSION

PLAYER 1

(ASK THE OTHER PLAYER(S) TO
CHOOSE QUESTION 1 OR QUESTION 2)

A = WOULD YOU RATHER

BRUSH YOUR TEETH WITH SNAIL SLIME

 OR

EAT A TIN OF DOG FOOD?

B = WOULD YOU RATHER

SING THE NATIONAL ANTHEM IN FRONT OF MILLIONS OF PEOPLE

 OR

DANCE LIKE A CHICKEN FOR THE ENTIRE DAY AT SCHOOL?

Ewwww! VERSION

PLAYER 2

(ASK THE OTHER PLAYER(S) TO
CHOOSE QUESTION 1 OR QUESTION 2)

A — WOULD YOU RATHER

SMELL LIKE CHICKEN CURRY FOR THE REST OF YOUR LIFE

 OR

SMELL LIKE GARLIC FOR THE REST OF YOUR LIFE?

B — WOULD YOU RATHER

GET COVERED IN 100 RAW EGGS

 OR

GET 100 TINS OF BEANS OPENED AND THROWN ALL OVER YOUR BODY?

Ewwww! VERSION

PLAYER 1

(ASK THE OTHER PLAYER(S) TO
CHOOSE QUESTION 1 OR QUESTION 2)

A WOULD YOU RATHER

GO OUT TO SEE YOUR FRIENDS SOAKED IN MAYONNAISE

 OR

GO OUT TO SEE YOUR FRIENDS AND BE SOAKED IN TOMATO SAUCE?

B WOULD YOU RATHER

SMELL LIKE CANNED TUNA

 OR

SMELL LIKE ROTTEN EGG?

Ewwww!
VERSION

PLAYER 2

(ASK THE OTHER PLAYER(S) TO
CHOOSE QUESTION 1 OR QUESTION 2)

A WOULD YOU RATHER

WOULD YOU SWIM IN A POOL WHERE YOU KNOW PEOPLE HAVE PEED

 OR

EAT YOUR OWN TOENAILS?

B WOULD YOU RATHER

SMELL ROTTING SEWAGE FOR A DAY

 OR

SLEEP IN A ROOM FILLED WITH CLOWNS?

Ewwww! VERSION

PLAYER 1

(ASK THE OTHER PLAYER(S) TO
CHOOSE QUESTION 1 OR QUESTION 2)

A WOULD YOU RATHER

HAVE THE FLU FOR A YEAR

 OR

FART OVER A THOUSAND TIMES A DAY FOR A MONTH?

B WOULD YOU RATHER

WAKE UP TO YOUR BED FILLED WITH BUGS

 OR

WAKE UP AND FIND YOUR BED FILLED WITH BEES?

Ewwww! VERSION

PLAYER 2

(ASK THE OTHER PLAYER(S) TO
CHOOSE QUESTION 1 OR QUESTION 2)

A **WOULD YOU RATHER**

RIDE A HORSE TO SCHOOL EVERY DAY

 OR

GO TO SCHOOL IN A BIG TRUCK?

B **WOULD YOU RATHER**

EAT ONLY PEANUT BUTTER AND JELLY SANDWICHES FOR A YEAR

 OR

EAT ONLY SUSHI FOR A YEAR?

PLAYER 1

(ASK THE OTHER PLAYER(S) TO
CHOOSE QUESTION 1 OR QUESTION 2)

WOULD YOU RATHER

HAVE NO EARS AND AN EXTRA-LONG NOSE

 OR

HAVE A NORMAL SIZE NOSE AND FIVE BIG PAIRS OF EARS THAT STICK OUT?

WOULD YOU RATHER

JOIN THE CIRCUS

 OR

JOIN BALLET SCHOOL?

Ewwww! VERSION

PLAYER 2

(ASK THE OTHER PLAYER(S) TO
CHOOSE QUESTION 1 OR QUESTION 2)

A = WOULD YOU RATHER

BE THE RICHEST PERSON
IN THE WORLD AND LOOK
LIKE A MONSTER

 OR

LOOK LIKE YOURSELF
AND BE POOR ?

B = WOULD YOU RATHER

HAVE A COOL DRINK
THAT TASTES LIKE
PUMPKIN

 OR

HAVE A COOL DRINK
THAT TASTES LIKE EGGS?

Ewwww!
VERSION

PLAYER 1

(ASK THE OTHER PLAYER(S) TO
CHOOSE QUESTION 1 OR QUESTION 2)

WOULD YOU RATHER

A

LICK A TRASH CAN

 OR

SHOWER IN STICKY OLIVE OIL?

WOULD YOU RATHER

B

DRINK JUICE WITH PICKLED FISH IN

 OR

DRINK JUICE WITH SOMEONE ELSE'S SPIT IN IT?

Ewwww! VERSION

PLAYER 2

(ASK THE OTHER PLAYER(S) TO
CHOOSE QUESTION 1 OR QUESTION 2)

A = WOULD YOU RATHER

HAVE FLEAS CRAWLING ALL OVER YOUR BODY

 OR

HAVE LICE IN YOUR HAIR?

B = WOULD YOU RATHER

HAVE ELEVEN TOES AND NINE FINGERS

 OR

HAVE ELEVEN FINGERS AND NINE TOES?

Ewwww! VERSION

PLAYER 1

(ASK THE OTHER PLAYER(S) TO
CHOOSE QUESTION 1 OR QUESTION 2)

A — WOULD YOU RATHER

HAVE A JUMPING CASTLE
IN YOUR BACK GARDEN

 OR

HAVE YOUR OWN PET
DINOSAUR ?

B — WOULD YOU RATHER

BE FRIENDS WITH A
VAMPIRE

 OR

BE FRIENDS WITH A REAL
WITCH ?

Ewwww! VERSION

PLAYER 2

(ASK THE OTHER PLAYER(S) TO *CHOOSE QUESTION 1 OR QUESTION 2*)

A WOULD YOU RATHER

HAVE PURPLE DOTS ALL OVER YOUR FACE

 OR

PICTURES OF FRUIT AND VEGETABLES ON YOUR LEGS?

B WOULD YOU RATHER

BE A FLYING DRAGON

 OR

BE AN INVISIBLE GHOST?

Ewwww! VERSION

PLAYER 1

(ASK THE OTHER PLAYER(S) TO
CHOOSE QUESTION 1 OR QUESTION 2)

A — WOULD YOU RATHER

FIND A DEAD DOG IN YOUR ROOM THAT WAS HALF EATEN

OR

FIND TEN DEAD RATS IN YOUR ROOM?

B — WOULD YOU RATHER

HAVE ROTTEN TEETH THAT ARE TURNING BLACK

OR

HAVE GREEN EARS THAT ARE FALLING OFF?

Ewwww!
VERSION

PLAYER 2

(ASK THE OTHER PLAYER(S) TO
CHOOSE QUESTION 1 OR QUESTION 2)

A — WOULD YOU RATHER

SWALLOW A GOLDFISH THAT WAS ALIVE

OR

SPEND AN HOUR COVERED IN SNAKES?

B — WOULD YOU RATHER

EAT PICKLED CUCUMBER FLAVOURED CHOCOLATE

OR

A CHEESE BURGER THAT IS COVERED IN MILK?

Ewwww! VERSION

PLAYER 1

(ASK THE OTHER PLAYER(S) TO
CHOOSE QUESTION 1 OR QUESTION 2)

A | WOULD YOU RATHER

SMELL A STRANGERS THROW UP

 OR

SMELL THE TOILET AFTER A STRANGER HAD MADE A BIG POOP?

B | WOULD YOU RATHER

GO TO THE DENTIST TWENTY TIMES A YEAR

 OR

GO TO THE DOCTOR TWENTY TIMES A YEAR?

Ewwww! VERSION

PLAYER 2

(ASK THE OTHER PLAYER(S) TO
CHOOSE QUESTION 1 OR QUESTION 2)

WOULD YOU RATHER

A

EAT CHOCOLATE CAKE COVERED IN BLOOD

OR

EAT A PIECE OF CHICKEN THAT FELL ON THE FLOOR AND WAS COVERED IN DIRT?

WOULD YOU RATHER

B

YOUR TEACHER TURNED INTO A COW

OR

YOUR TEACHER TURNED INTO A SQUIRREL?

Ewwww! VERSION

PLAYER 1

(ASK THE OTHER PLAYER(S) TO
CHOOSE QUESTION 1 OR QUESTION 2)

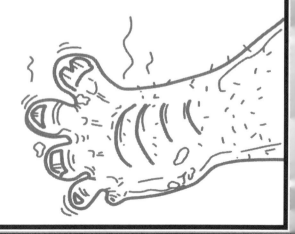

A WOULD YOU RATHER

EAT YOUR HOMEWORK

 OR

DO EXTRA HOMEWORK EVERY DAY FOR THE REST OF YOUR LIFE?

B WOULD YOU RATHER

STUDY VAMPIRES INSTEAD OF GEOGRAPHY

 OR

STUDY WITCHES INSTEAD OF SCIENCE?

Ewwww! VERSION

PLAYER 2

(ASK THE OTHER PLAYER(S) TO
CHOOSE QUESTION 1 OR QUESTION 2)

A = WOULD YOU RATHER

EAT A CAKE THAT HAD OTHER PEOPLES HAIR IN IT

 OR

EAT A CHOCOLATE THAT HAD OTHER PEOPLE'S NAILS IN IT?

B = WOULD YOU RATHER

HAVE A NOSEBLEED EVERY TIME YOU ATE CHOCOLATE

 OR

NEVER EAT CHOCOLATE AGAIN AND NOT HAVE A NOSEBLEED?

Ewwww! VERSION

PLAYER 1

(ASK THE OTHER PLAYER(S) TO
CHOOSE QUESTION 1 OR QUESTION 2)

A WOULD YOU RATHER

BE COVERED IN ANTS

BE COVERED IN CATERPILLARS?

B WOULD YOU RATHER

HAVE A BLACK TONGUE AND RED TEETH

HAVE NO TEETH AND NO TONGUE?

Ewwww! VERSION

PLAYER 2

(ASK THE OTHER PLAYER(S) TO
CHOOSE QUESTION 1 OR QUESTION 2)

A **WOULD YOU RATHER**

LICK THE BOTTOM PART OF A STRANGERS SHOE

OR

LICK THE TOILET SEAT AT YOUR NEAREST MCDONALD'S?

B **WOULD YOU RATHER**

HAVE A CATS HEAD AND A HUMAN BODY

OR

HAVE A CAT'S BODY AND A HUMAN HEAD?

Ewwww! VERSION

PLAYER 1

(ASK THE OTHER PLAYER(S) TO
CHOOSE QUESTION 1 OR QUESTION 2)

A = WOULD YOU RATHER

BE GRANTED THREE WISHES FROM A GENIE IN A BOTTLE

 OR

BE GRANTED A FULL DAY OF UNLIMITED WISHES FROM A FAIRY GODMOTHER?

B = WOULD YOU RATHER

LICK SOMEONE ELSE'S SCABS

 OR

ICK A DOG'S EAR FOR TWO MINUTES WITHOUT STOPPING?

Ewwww! VERSION

PLAYER 2

(ASK THE OTHER PLAYER(S) TO
CHOOSE QUESTION 1 OR QUESTION 2)

A = WOULD YOU RATHER

BE A POLICEMAN

 OR

A FIRE-FIGHTER?

B = WOULD YOU RATHER

BE SUPERMAN FOR A DAY

 OR

HAVE WINGS FOR THE REST OF YOUR LIFE?

PLAYER 1

(ASK THE OTHER PLAYER(S) TO
CHOOSE QUESTION 1 OR QUESTION 2)

A — WOULD YOU RATHER

GET COVERED IN OLD SMELLY BANANAS

 OR

GET COVERED IN MUD?

B — WOULD YOU RATHER

DRINK DIRTY SEA WATER

 OR

DRINK VERY OLD COW'S MILK THAT HAS BEEN SITTING IN THE SUN FOR WEEKS?

Ewwww! VERSION

PLAYER 2

(ASK THE OTHER PLAYER(S) TO
CHOOSE QUESTION 1 OR QUESTION 2)

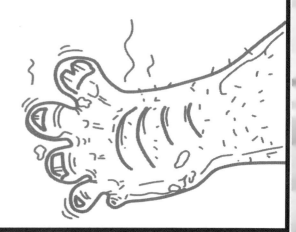

A WOULD YOU RATHER

HAVE THREE EYES ON YOUR FACE

 OR

HAVE THREE LEGS?

B WOULD YOU RATHER

HAVE TEN BROTHERS AND NO SISTERS

 OR

TEN SISTERS AND NO BROTHERS?

Ewwww! VERSION

PLAYER 1

(ASK THE OTHER PLAYER(S) TO
CHOOSE QUESTION 1 OR QUESTION 2)

A  WOULD YOU RATHER

THROW UP WORMS

 OR

EAT FLIES?

B WOULD YOU RATHER

USE YOUR MATHS TEACHER'S TOOTHBRUSH

 OR

WALK AROUND WITH RAINBOW AND UNICORN SLIPPERS ON FOR A WEEK?

Ewwww! VERSION

PLAYER 2

(ASK THE OTHER PLAYER(S) TO
CHOOSE QUESTION 1 OR QUESTION 2)

A = WOULD YOU RATHER

EAT A DEAD FLY

 OR

A WORM THAT'S ALIVE ?

B = WOULD YOU RATHER

YOUR PARENTS PICKED YOU UP FROM SCHOOL EVERY DAY IN AN ICE CREAM TRUCK

 OR

YOUR PARENTS PICKED YOU UP FROM SCHOOL EVERY DAY IN A POLICE CAR?

Ewwww! VERSION

PLAYER 1

(ASK THE OTHER PLAYER(S) TO CHOOSE QUESTION 1 OR QUESTION 2)

A WOULD YOU RATHER

HAVE BLACK EYES AND PINK HAIR

OR

WOULD YOU HAVE PINK EYES AND BLACK HAIR?

B WOULD YOU RATHER

TURN INTO A WEREWOLF AT MIDNIGHT

OR

TURN INTO A PUMPKIN AT MIDNIGHT?

Ewwww! VERSION

PLAYER 2

(ASK THE OTHER PLAYER(S) TO
CHOOSE QUESTION 1 OR QUESTION 2)

A WOULD YOU RATHER

DO 100 PUSH-UPS EVERY SINGLE DAY

 OR

WALK UP 100 STAIRS EVERY SINGLE DAY?

B WOULD YOU RATHER

BECOME FAMOUS FOR PLAYING THE PIANO WELL

 OR

BECOME FAMOUS FOR BAKING THE BEST CHOCOLATE CAKE IN THE WORLD?

Ewwww! VERSION

PLAYER 1

(ASK THE OTHER PLAYER(S) TO
CHOOSE QUESTION 1 OR QUESTION 2)

WOULD YOU RATHER

WASH YOUR HAIR WITH TOMATO SAUCE

OR

WASH YOUR HAIR WITH GARLIC SAUCE?

WOULD YOU RATHER

SWIM IN A POOL WITH FLEAS

OR

SWIM IN A POOL FILLED WITH WORMS?

Ewwww! VERSION

PLAYER 2

(ASK THE OTHER PLAYER(S) TO
CHOOSE QUESTION 1 OR QUESTION 2)

A WOULD YOU RATHER

EAT A PICKLED CUCUMBER AND WORM SANDWICH

 OR

EAT A PINEAPPLE AND RAT PIZZA?

B WOULD YOU RATHER

WEAR SOMEONE ELSE'S UNDERWEAR FOR A YEAR

 OR

GO WITHOUT EVER WEARING UNDERWEAR FOR A YEAR?

Ewwww! VERSION

PLAYER 1

(ASK THE OTHER PLAYER(S) TO
CHOOSE QUESTION 1 OR QUESTION 2)

A = WOULD YOU RATHER

HAVE LONG HAIR THAT IS SO LONG THAT IT RUNS DOWN TO YOUR ANKLES

 OR

HAVE NO HAIR AT ALL?

B = WOULD YOU RATHER

KISS TEN FROGS A DAY EVERY DAY FOR A YEAR

 OR

LIVE AS A FROG FOR SIX MONTHS?

Ewwww! VERSION

PLAYER 2

(ASK THE OTHER PLAYER(S) TO
CHOOSE QUESTION 1 OR QUESTION 2)

A WOULD YOU RATHER

OWN YOUR OWN ZOO

 OR

BECOME A PILOT?

B WOULD YOU RATHER

HAVE YOUR OWN PET DRAGON

 OR

HAVE YOUR OWN PET GOAT?

Ewwww! VERSION

PLAYER 1

(ASK THE OTHER PLAYER(S) TO
CHOOSE QUESTION 1 OR QUESTION 2)

A — WOULD YOU RATHER

HAVE FIVE EYES AND NO FEET

 OR

FIVE FEET AND NO EYES?

B — WOULD YOU RATHER

PUT YOUR FACE IN A WARM BOWL OF MILK AND WORMS

 OR

PUT YOUR FEET IN A TANK WITH FROGS?

Ewwww! VERSION

PLAYER 2

(ASK THE OTHER PLAYER(S) TO
CHOOSE QUESTION 1 OR QUESTION 2)

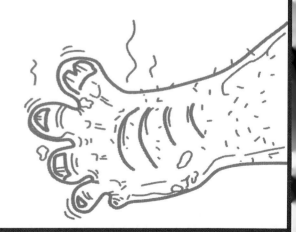

A WOULD YOU RATHER

HAVE YOUR HAIR TURN ALL WHITE

OR

YOUR FINGERS TURN ROTTEN AND FALL OFF ONE BY ONE?

B WOULD YOU RATHER

BECOME A FAMOUS AUTHOR

OR

BECOME A FAMOUS TV PRESENTER?

Ewwww! VERSION

PLAYER 1

(ASK THE OTHER PLAYER(S) TO
CHOOSE QUESTION 1 OR QUESTION 2)

A = WOULD YOU RATHER

EAT YOUR OWN NOSE HAIRS

 OR

EAT YOUR OWN EAR WAX?

B = WOULD YOU RATHER

EAT FOOD THAT YOU KNOW WILL MAKE YOU FART REALLY BAD FOR A WEEK

 **OR**

DRINK A PURPLE POISON THAT WOULD MAKE YOU THROW UP?

Ewwww! VERSION

PLAYER 2

(ASK THE OTHER PLAYER(S) TO
CHOOSE QUESTION 1 OR QUESTION 2)

A — WOULD YOU RATHER

DRINK A SMOOTHIE OF MUD AND RABBIT POOP

 OR

WOULD YOU DRINK A SMOOTHIE OF DOG WEE AND WORMS?

B — WOULD YOU RATHER

SIT IN A ROOM FOR A DAY WITH A RAW HALF OF A PIG'S HEAD

 OR

SIT IN A ROOM FOR A DAY WITH 100 COCKROACHES THAT WERE ALIVE?

Ewwww! VERSION

PLAYER 1

(ASK THE OTHER PLAYER(S) TO
CHOOSE QUESTION 1 OR QUESTION 2)

A — WOULD YOU RATHER

GO ON HOLIDAY TO DISNEYLAND FOR THREE DAYS

HAVE NO SCHOOL FOR 2 MONTHS?

B — WOULD YOU RATHER

BE BEST FRIENDS WITH A LION

BE BEST FRIENDS WITH A CHEETAH?

Ewwww! VERSION

PLAYER 2

(ASK THE OTHER PLAYER(S) TO
CHOOSE QUESTION 1 OR QUESTION 2*)*

A WOULD YOU RATHER

SLEEP WITH ICE-CREAM IN YOUR BED

 OR

SLEEP WITH ORANGE JUICE SPILT ALL OVER YOUR SHEETS?

B WOULD YOU RATHER

PLAY MONOPOLY WITH WITCHES

 OR

PLAY CHESS WITH VAMPIRES?

Ewwww! VERSION

PLAYER 1

(ASK THE OTHER PLAYER(S) TO
CHOOSE QUESTION 1 OR QUESTION 2)

A WOULD YOU RATHER

WIN TEN HOUSES

 OR

WIN YOUR OWN ISLAND?

B WOULD YOU RATHER

NEVER EAT POPCORN AGAIN

 OR

NEVER EAT FRIED CHICKEN AGAIN?

Ewwww! VERSION

PLAYER 2

(ASK THE OTHER PLAYER(S) TO
CHOOSE QUESTION 1 OR QUESTION 2)

A WOULD YOU RATHER

SMELL UNDER A VERY DIRTY PERSON'S FOOT

 OR

SMELL A DOG'S BUM?

B WOULD YOU RATHER

SWALLOW A HAIRY CATERPILLAR ALIVE

 OR

HOLD A SNAKE FOR TEN FULL MINUTES?

Made in the USA
Columbia, SC
05 June 2022

61358054R00057